WE BOTH READ™

Parent's Introduction

We Both Read is the first series of books designed to invite parents and children to share the reading of a story by taking turns reading aloud. This "shared reading" innovation, which was developed in conjunction with early reading specialists, invites parents to read the more sophisticated text on the left-hand pages, while children are encouraged to read the right-hand pages, which have been written at one of three early reading levels.

Reading aloud is one of the most important activities parents can share with their child to assist their reading development. However, *We Both Read* goes beyond reading *to* a child and allows parents to share reading *with* a child. *We Both Read* is so powerful and effective because it combines two key elements in learning: "showing" (the parent reads) and "doing" (the child reads). The result is not only faster reading development for the child, but a much more enjoyable and enriching experience for both!

Most of the words used in the child's text should be familiar to them. Others can easily be sounded out. An occasional difficult word will be first introduced in the parent's text, distinguished with **bold lettering**. Pointing out these words, as you read them, will help familiarize them to your child. You may also find it helpful to read the entire book aloud yourself the first time, then invite your child to participate on the second reading. Also note that the parent's text is preceded by a "talking parent" icon: ☺ ; and the child's text is preceded by a "talking child" icon: ☺ .

We Both Read books is a fun, easy way to encourage and help your child to read — and a wonderful way to start your child off on a lifetime of reading enjoyment!

We Both Read: The Three Little Pigs

We Both Read™ is a trademark of Treasure Bay, Inc.

Published by Treasure Bay, Inc.
50 Horgan Ave., Suite 12
Redwood City, CA 94061 USA

PRINTED IN SINGAPORE

Library of Congress Catalog Card Number: 98-60703

Hardcover ISBN 1-891327-05-4
Softcover ISBN 1-891327-09-7

FIRST EDITION

We Both Read™ Books
Patent Pending

WE BOTH READ ™

The Three Little Pigs

Adapted by Dev Ross

Illustrated by Erin Marie Mauterer

TREASURE BAY

There once was a mother Pig with so many little Pigs that they were always under one foot or another. So she told the three oldest to go out into the world.

And when they asked if they could stay, she said,

 "No, no!
You have to go!"

Now the three little Pigs each needed a home, but building a **house** was a lot of work! And the first little Pig would rather watch TV.

So when he found some hay, he thought he had it made.

🐷 "A **house** of hay!
What a good day!"

The first little Pig built his house as fast as he
could. When he was done, he felt he had
earned his **rest.** So he turned on his TV, and
said with a sigh,

"Now I can sit
and **rest** a bit."

But the Wolf was watching.

Now this was not a nice Wolf. This Wolf was bad. But he knocked politely on the door. The **little** Pig's TV, however, was too loud to hear, so the Wolf had to shout,

"Little Pig,
little Pig,
let me come in!"

This, the Pig heard.
But he did not want to let the Wolf in.
So he yelled back, "Not by the hair of my chinny, chin chin!"

This did not make the Wolf happy.

He was bad
and he was mad.

So the Wolf shouted back, "Then I'll huff and I'll puff and I'll blow your house in!"

And that's just what he did.

 "Oh no! Oh no!
I have to go!"

And with that, the little Pig ran away! But when he came back to get his TV – the Wolf gobbled him up.

And that was the end of the first little Pig.

"A Pig to eat.
How sweet!"

Now the second little Pig did not want to build a house either. He would much rather eat.
So when he stumbled upon a pile of **sticks**, he thought he had it made.

 "A house of **sticks**
is what I pick."

The second little Pig built his house as fast as he could. When he was done, he felt sure he had earned a **treat**, so he opened his refrigerator and said with glee,

 "I want to eat.
I want a **treat!**"

But the Wolf was watching.

So up to the door he leaped and knocked politely. The second little Pig, however, was too busy eating to hear, so the Wolf had to shout,

"Little Pig,
little Pig,
let me come in!"

This, the Pig heard.

But he did not want to let the Wolf in. So with his mouth full he mumbled, "Not by the hair of my chinny, chin chin!"

This made the Wolf mad.

He was bad
and he was mad!

So the Wolf shouted back, "Then I'll huff and I'll puff and I'll blow your house in!"

And that's just what he did.

"Oh no! Oh no!
I want to go!"

And with that, the little Pig ran away. But when he came back to get his favorite sucker – the Wolf gobbled him up.

And that was the end of the second little Pig.

 "That little Pig
was big!"

Now the third little Pig *wanted* to build a house. So when he found a pile of **bricks**, he knew just what to do.

"A house of **brick**
is very thick."

The third little Pig built his house
carefully. Then he washed his dishes and
swept the floor. And when he was **done**,
he looked around and said,

"I am **done.**
That was fun!"

But the Wolf was watching.

Up to the door he marched and knocked very loud. The third little Pig, however, was too *smart* to answer, so the Wolf had to shout,

"Little Pig,
little Pig,
let me come in!"

This, the Pig most certainly heard.
He checked every lock so the Wolf couldn't break in before he shouted, "Not by the hair of my chinny, chin chin!"

This made the Wolf *furious*!

He was bad
and he was mad!

So the Wolf yelled, "Then I'll huff and I'll puff and I'll blow your house in!"

So he huffed and he puffed. And he puffed and he huffed.

But he could not blow the brick house down.

The Wolf said,

"This brick
is thick!"

So the Wolf stopped huffing and puffing and tried getting in through the chimney instead.

This was not a good idea.

See the pot?
It is hot!

That Wolf landed right in the big old pot! And because he made such a delicious soup — the third little Pig gobbled him up.

And that was the end of *that* bad Wolf.

And how, you may ask, did the bad Wolf taste?

Not bad!
Not bad!

The End

If you liked
The Three Little Pigs, **here are two other**
We Both Read™ **Books you are sure to enjoy!**

In this delightfully funny retelling of the classic story, the emperor hires two tailors to make him an elegant new set of clothes. The tailors say the clothes are magical and that some people will think the clothes are invisible. Can you guess what happens when the emperor wears his new clothes?